HALL OF FAME

THE ALPACAS

READY, PACK, GO!

Ruth Chan

HARPER
An Imprint of HarperCollins*Publishers*

Library of Congress Control Number: 2019957888
ISBN 978-0-06-290951-0

The artist used acrylic, gouache, and charcoal pencils
to create the digital illustrations for this book.
Typography by Chelsea C. Donaldson
20 21 22 23 24 RTLO 10 9 8 7 6 5 4 3 2 1
❖
First Edition

To Mom and Dad, for being my Alpactory

—R.C.

Are you going somewhere new
and excited for your adventure?

But no matter how hard you try, you just don't feel ready?
Are you worried you'll pack the wrong things
for your sleepover?

Yes.

Or that you won't have
enough pencils for your
first day of school?

Definitely.

Is there just too much stuff to
pack for your camping trip?

Without a doubt.

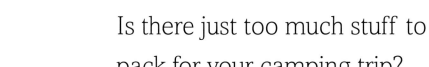

Don't worry!

The Alpactory's here to help!

At the Alpactory,
we know just what you'll need,
guaranteed!

We'll pick and pack all the right things.
And then you'll be on your way.

Are you worried you'll feel lonely?

Don't fret! We've got the best books to keep you company.

Or maybe you're afraid of the dark?

Here's a flashlight to shine the way.

We can even pack a bit of home for you
so you won't forget that home misses you too.

Next we'll pack some clothes that we've tested in all kinds of weather—

so you're never too hot . . .

and never too cold.

Want to stay dry in the rain? Or wet in the bathtub?
We've got that figured out too!

And snacks!
We'll pack the wobbliest and crunchiest and slurpiest snacks around.

Yum!

We'll pack things that bounce

and things that roar,

and then we'll even pack some more!

We'll pack and pack
and pack until …

WAIT!

Thank you, but this is too much stuff.

Yeah! I only need
one toothbrush.

And just these
two pencils.

Hey!

Maybe we've been ready . . .

all along!

Hmm . . .
I think you're right!

After all, you are brave and kind and funny.

You already had everything you needed!

Wherever you go, whether close or far,
you'll be ready.

So get excited
to try new things,

to make new friends …

and to see what's out there.

Until you're back home

and ready to do it all again.